Love is in the Hair

By
Syrus Marcus Ware

The night before the Very Big Day -
the day her parents brought her new baby sister home -
Carter woke up at 3:33 am, and she
could NOT get back to sleep.

She went to her Mom and Dad's room
and then remembered...
they were at the hospital!

She called out:
"Uncle Marcus? Uncle Jeff? I CAN'T SLEEP!"

No one answered.

So she went to the living room and found them on the sofa bed, fast asleep.

Carter said "I can't sleep," a few more times, until Uncle Marcus woke up.

Uncle Marcus sent Uncle Jeff to make
some warm milk in the kitchen,
and walked down the hall to Carter's room.

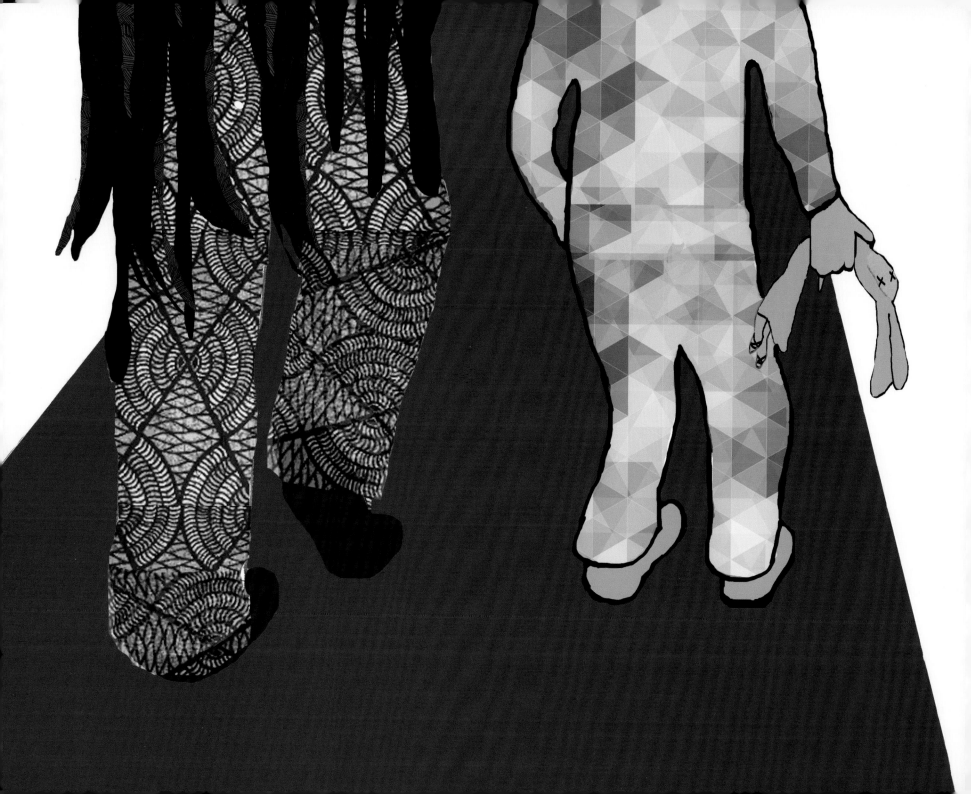

"Carter!" said Uncle Marcus, "You need to try to sleep."
Remember little one, we need to get lots of sleep tonight
so that we're rested for the big day tomorrow!

Your new sister will be here soon,
and we want to be awake to meet her."

"I can't sleep,"
Carter complained.
"I'm too excited!
Could you tell me a story?"

Uncle Marcus settled onto the edge of the bed, carefully moving his hair out from under him as he sat down.

Carter looked at her uncle's hair with wonder.
It was full of beads, fabric, shells and jewels,
memories and stories and magic.

"Okay, my little one," said Uncle Marcus, "climb up here.
What story do you want to hear?"

"What is this bead from?" Carter asked, and smiled.
She knew this story and liked it best of all.

Uncle Marcus held it up, and said "This bead is from a very
special day 4 years ago, when you were born!"

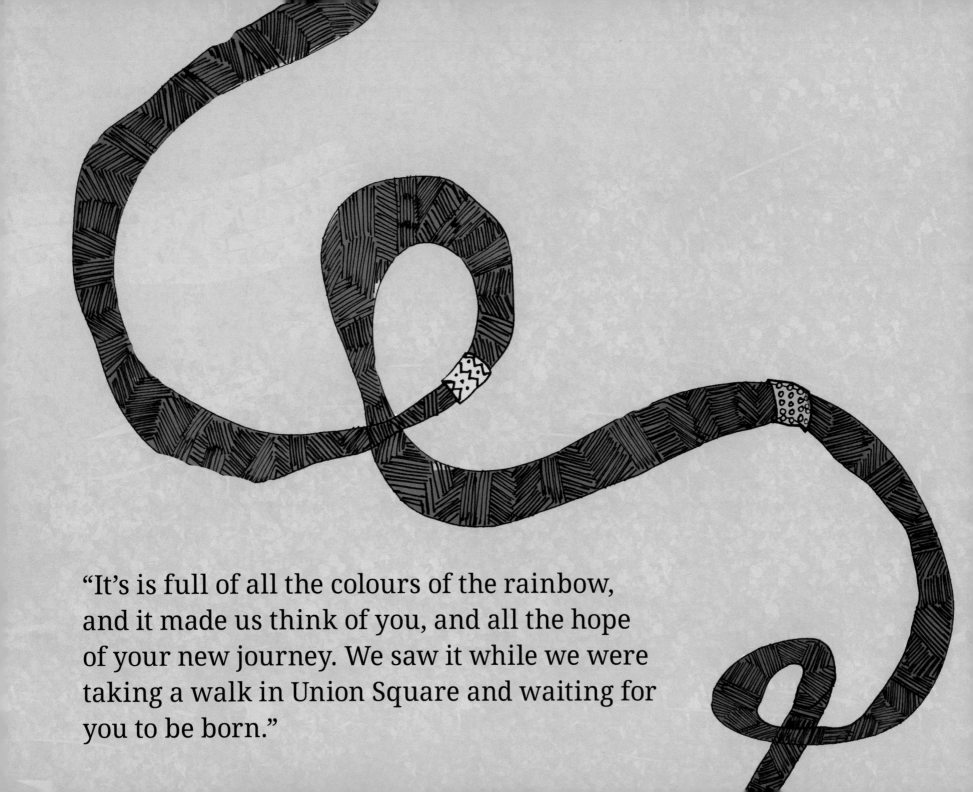

"It's is full of all the colours of the rainbow,
and it made us think of you, and all the hope
of your new journey. We saw it while we were
taking a walk in Union Square and waiting for
you to be born."

"There was an artist selling handmade glass beads, and I knew right away which one would remind me of you forever," said Uncle Marcus.

"What about this one?" asked Carter.

Uncle Marcus said "This piece of metal? It's from a music festival I went to long ago, before your Mom even knew your Dad. I met Uncle Jeff at that festival…"

"I stopped to buy this metal bead. He was selling metal bracelets, and we started talking. I've worn it in my hair ever since."

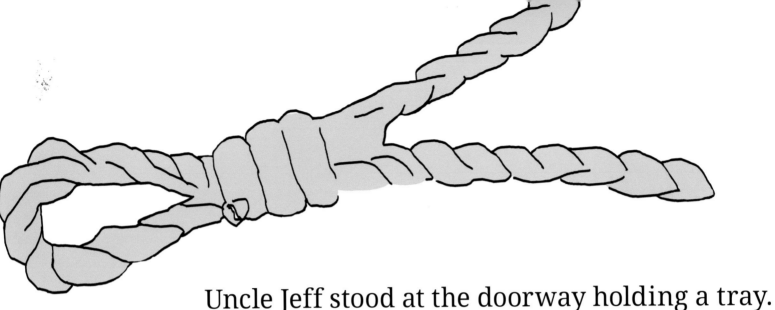

Uncle Jeff stood at the doorway holding a tray.

"Did I hear a request for warm milk?" Uncle Jeff asked. He passed a warm cup to Uncle Marcus and to Carter.

Then, Uncle Jeff said: "But you didn't buy the bracelet, I gave it to you - and a woven bracelet, too! I liked you from the first moment."

Uncle Marcus laughed. They always remembered parts of the story differently.

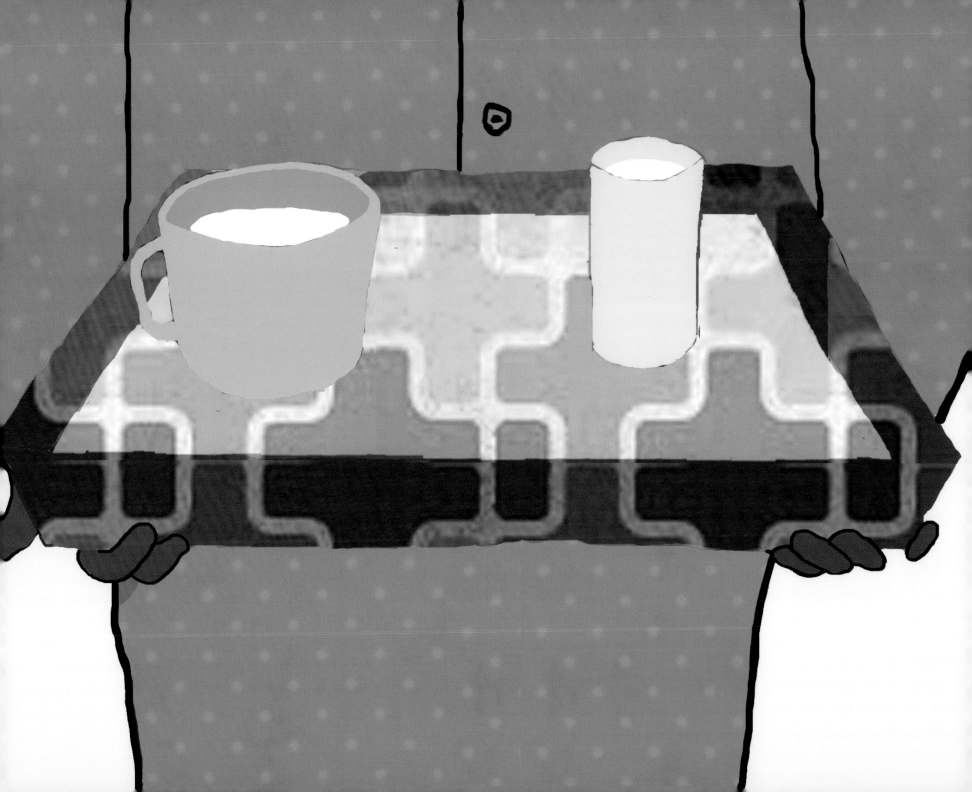

"Yes! And thats why you have this story in your hair! This pink is from that bracelet, right Uncle Jeff?!"

Carter held up dreadlocks with a pink thread running through them.

"That thread is from the day we decided to be each other's family," said Uncle Jeff. "We wove some of the threads from the bracelet into Uncle Marcus' hair."

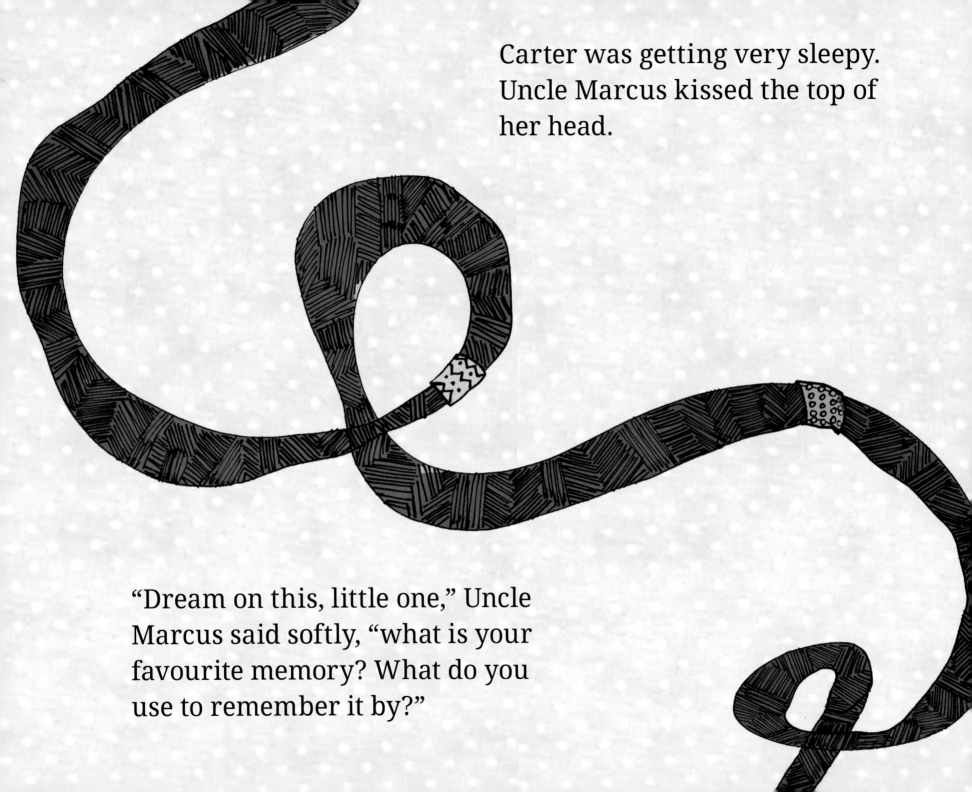

Carter was getting very sleepy.
Uncle Marcus kissed the top of
her head.

"Dream on this, little one," Uncle
Marcus said softly, "what is your
favourite memory? What do you
use to remember it by?"